There Once Was a Man Named Michael Finnegan

The last two words of the song, "Begin-igan," invite
the listeners to start singing the song all over again.

Key of G

G

There once was a man named Mich - ael Fin - ne - gan,

D   G

he had whis - kers on his chin - i - gan, shaved them off and

G   D   G

they grew in - i - gan, poor old Mich - ael Fin - ne - gan, be - gin - i - gan.

To Dorothy Gray Hoberman, with love
— M. A. H.

To Becky, Wendy, and Willy
— N. B. W.

Text copyright © 2001 by Mary Ann Hoberman
Illustrations copyright © 2001 by Nadine Bernard Westcott

First Edition

Library of Congress Cataloging-in-Publication Data

Hoberman, Mary Ann.
   There once was a man named Michael Finnegan / adapted by Mary Ann Hoberman ; illustrated by Nadine
Bernard Westcott.—1st ed.
     p. cm.
   Summary: An elaborated version of the repetitive children's song about a man who creates quite a "din-igan"
playing the "violin-igan."
   ISBN 0-316-36301-4
   1. Children's songs—Texts. [1. Songs.] 1. Westcott, Nadine Bernard, ill. II. Title.
PZ8.3.H66 Th 2000
782.42164'0268—dc21
[E]   99-057266

10 9 8 7 6 5 4 3 2

TWP

Printed in Singapore

The illustrations in this book were done in watercolors and ink.
The text was set in Goudy Sans Medium, and the display type is handlettered.

There Once Was a Man Named Michael Finnegan

Adapted by
Mary Ann Hoberman

Illustrated by
Nadine Bernard Westcott

Megan Tingley Books

LITTLE, BROWN and COMPANY
Boston New York London

There once was a man named Michael Finnegan,
He had whiskers on his chin-igan,
Shaved them off and they grew in-igan,
    Poor old Michael Finnegan, begin-igan.

This poor old man named Michael Finnegan
Dressed in rags to hide his skin-igan,
Held his pants up with a pin-igan,
Tattered Michael Finnegan, begin-igan.

Michael played the violin-igan,
Tucked it underneath his chin-igan,
Played so loud it was a sin-igan,
Noisy Michael Finnegan, begin-igan.

Every time that he'd start in-igan,
People kicked him in the shin-igan,
Said they'd pay to stop the din-igan
    Made by Michael Finnegan, begin-igan.

Michael then would pass his tin-igan,
People all put money in-igan,
All that money made him grin-igan,
    Rich old Michael Finnegan, begin-igan.

He bought a car and hopped right in-igan,
Drove it off and took a spin-igan,
Went to visit all his kin-igan,
　　Jolly Michael Finnegan, begin-igan.

They all asked him, "Where've you been-igan?
Glad to see you. Please come in-igan.
Will you play your violin-igan?
Dear old Michael Finnegan, begin-igan."

Michael took his violin-igan,
Tucked it underneath his chin-igan,
Tuned it up and started in-igan,
    Hopeful Michael Finnegan, begin-igan.

Everyone began to grin-igan,
"He's no better than he's been-igan,
Still can't play his violin-igan,
    Foolish Michael Finnegan, begin-igan."

Michael said, "I just can't win-igan.
No one likes my violin-igan,
I wish someone liked my din-igan."
  Gloomy Michael Finnegan, begin-igan.

Michael took another spin-igan,
Found a dog and named him Quinn-igan,
He had whiskers on his chin-igan,
Just like Michael Finnegan, begin-igan.

Michael and his new dog, Quinn-igan,
Took the money from their tin-igan,
Bought a house and moved right in-igan,
Merry Michael Finnegan, begin-igan.

Michael played his violin-igan,
When Quinn heard it, he joined in-igan,
He enjoyed the awful din-igan
 Made by Michael Finnegan, begin-igan.

Michael takes his violin-igan,
Quinn sits up and starts to grin-igan,
Kisses Michael on his chin-igan,
   Happy Michael Finnegan, begin-igan!